Dinosaur School

DINOSAUR COLORS

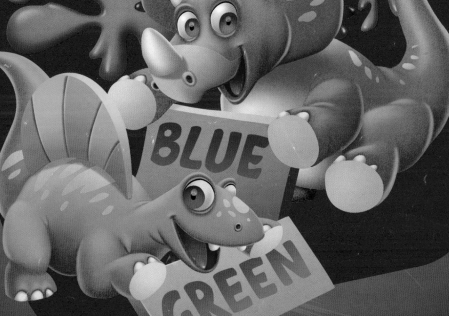

BLUE

GREEN

Please visit our website, www.garethstevens.com. For a free color catalog of all our high-quality books, call toll free 1-800-542-2595 or fax 1-877-542-2596.

Library of Congress Cataloging-in-Publication Data

Library of Congress Cataloging-in-Publication Data

Saviola, Ava.
Dinosaur colors / Ava Saviola.
   p. cm. — (Dinosaur school)
ISBN 978-1-4339-7140-2 (pbk.)
ISBN 978-1-4339-7141-9 (6-pack)
ISBN 978-1-4339-7139-6 (library binding)
1. Dinosaurs—Juvenile literature. 2. Colors—Juvenile literature. I. Title.
QE861.5.S3449 2013
535.6—dc23
                                          2011042817

First Edition

Published in 2013 by
Gareth Stevens Publishing
111 East 14th Street, Suite 349
New York, NY 10003

Copyright © 2013 Gareth Stevens Publishing

Designer: Ben Gardner
Editor: Kerri O'Donnell

All illustrations by Planman Technologies

Printed in the United States of America

CPSIA compliance information: Batch #CS12GS: For further information contact Gareth Stevens, New York, New York at 1-800-542-2595.

DINOSAUR COLORS

BLUE

GREEN

By Ava Saviola

Gareth Stevens
Publishing

red

red dinosaur

red

red apple

orange

orange **dinosaur**

orange

orange **pumpkin**

7

yellow

yellow dinosaur

yellow

yellow **star**

green

green dinosaur

green

green **grass**

blue

blue dinosaur

blue

blue balloon

purple

purple dinosaur

purple

purple ball

pink

pink dinosaur

pink

pink **flower**

brown

brown dinosaur

brown

brown box

gray

gray dinosaur

gray

gray **elephant**

black

black dinosaur

black

black boots

Dinosaur Colors

red

orange

yellow

green

blue

purple

pink

brown

gray

black